panda series

**PANDA books are for first readers
beginning to make their own way
through books.**

No Shoes for Tom!

UNA LEAVY

• Pictures by Margaret Suggs •

THE O'BRIEN PRESS
DUBLIN

First published by The O'Brien Press Ltd.,
20 Victoria Road, Dublin 6, Ireland

ISBN: 0-86278-526-X

1 2 3 4 5 6 7 8 9 10
97 98 99 00 01 02 03 04 05 06

British Library Cataloguing-in-publication Data
A catalogue reference for this title is
available from the British Library.

The O'Brien Press receives assistance from
The Arts Council / An Chomhairle Ealaíon

Typesetting, layout, editing: The O'Brien Press Ltd.
Cover separations: Lithoset Ltd., Dublin
Printing: Cox & Wyman Ltd.

Can YOU spot the panda
hidden in the story?

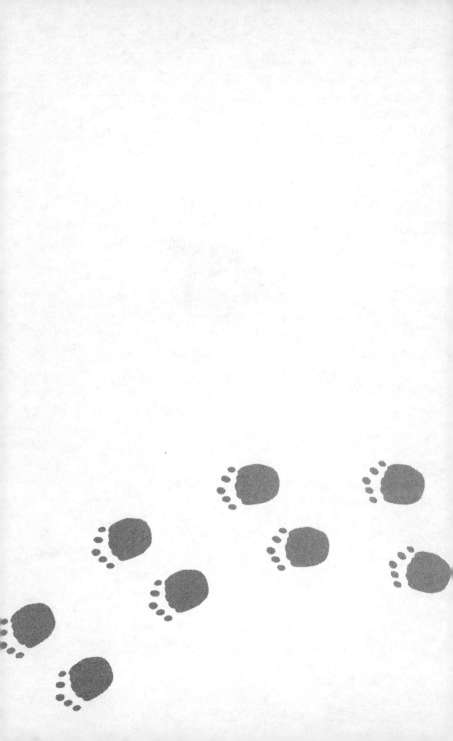

When Tom was a little baby
he did not wear shoes.
He loved to wiggle his toes
and put them in his mouth.
He had nice, pink toes.

One day when Tom
was a little older,
his mother put a pair of shoes
on him.

He did not like them at all.

He threw one at the clock,
and it fell to the floor
with a crash.

He threw the other shoe at Dad,
and it hit him on the nose.
Dad did not like that.

Every day for a long, long time,
Mum put a pair of shoes
on Tom.
Every day Tom took them
right off again.

Tom had such fun
with his bare toes
that he just would not
wear shoes or socks.

Sometimes a friendly puppy
came and licked his toes.
Tom liked that.

Dad took Tom to
a shoe shop in the town.
'You are a big boy now,'
said Dad. 'It is time
you started to wear shoes.'

The shopkeeper showed them
lots of shoes – **bright blue**
shoes, **shiny red** ones,
shoes with **straps**,
shoes with **laces**.

'**No**,' said Tom, when the
shopkeeper tried to fit
some shoes on him.
'I do not like the blue shoes
and I do not like the red ones.
I do not like the shoes
with straps.'

'I do not like the shoes
with laces.
**I do not like
any shoes at all**.'

Then Dad got very cross,
and the shopkeeper was
a little cross too.

But still Tom would not
wear any shoes.

Autumn came, and every day
Tom rustled his way
through the red and yellow
leaves in the wood.

Whenever it rained,
he squelched the black mud
between his toes and shaped it
into oozy wet hills.
Oh, it was such fun!

And then came winter.
One morning when Tom
looked out of the window
he saw big, fat snowflakes.

The trees were white.
The fields were white.
Everywhere was quite white.

Dad said, 'Will you help me
feed the calves, Tom?'
'Oh yes,' said Tom.
Mum wrapped him in his
warm coat and hat and gloves.

She did not say anything
about **shoes**.

But she winked at Dad
as they went out the door.

Tom put one pink toe

on the snow by the doorstep.

Oooh it was cold!

Dad took big long steps
and Tom had to run
to keep up with him.

Their feet made tracks
in the snow.

But oooh it was cold!

Little by little, Tom's pink toes
began to turn blue.
They got colder and colder,
and stiffer and stiffer.
Soon they were so cold
he could scarcely walk.

'Carry me, Daddy,' said Tom when he could bear the cold no longer.

'I'm sorry, Tom,' said Dad,
'I have to carry the bale of hay
for the calves. You must walk.'
'I cannot walk any more,'
cried Tom. 'My toes are
so cold.'

But Dad could not carry him,
so poor Tom had to trot along
in his bare feet until
Dad had fed the calves.
Then Dad took him up
in his arms and
carried him home.

When they got home
Mum took Tom on her lap.
She dried his tears
and his little cold, wet toes.
She gave him a big bowl
of hot porridge.

Then she said, 'Daddy,
will you bring that big box
from the chest, please?'

Dad brought the box and
when Tom opened it he found
a pair of beautiful, red shiny
boots!

Tom could hardly wait while
Mum put on his warm socks
and the **shiny red boots**.

He ran happily out
into the yard.
He kicked the snow
into the air
and threw snowballs
at the trees.

He built a big snowman,
and all the time his feet
stayed **dry** and **cosy**
and **warm**.

In the house,
Mum winked at Dad
and Dad winked back!

PANDA 1

MUCKEEN, THE PIG

Words and pictures by Fergus Lyons

Muckeen loves his farm and the big bucket of
sloppy stuff he gets for his dinner. But what
happens when he is taken to the market? Will
he ever see his home again?

PANDA 3

RIBBIT, RIBBIT!

ANNE MARIE HERRON
Pictures by Stephen Hall

'Ribbit, ribbit,' says Freddy. 'I'm a frog!'
Everyone laughs. But by the end of the week
they are all fed up with it. How can they get
him to be a boy again? Polly has the answer!

FIREMAN SINEAD!

ANNA DONOVAN
Pictures by Susan Cooper

Sinead wants to be a fireman. She practises and
practises. Tom thinks she's silly. Only boys can
be firemen anyway, he tells her. Is that true?
Sinead is not sure. But when a real fire happens
she gets a big surprise.

AMY'S WONDERFUL NEST

GORDON SNELL
Pictures by Fergus Lyons

Poor little Amy has fallen from the nest.
How will she manage to build a new one for
herself? Amy comes up with the most
amazing nest ever.